MW01101415

Contents

Birbal Acts Like a Child

Birbal reached the court quite late one day. Akbar inquired the reason for his delay. Birbal replied, "Your Majesty! My son was crying. It was tough to console him."

Akbar retorted, "Oh, Birbal! How difficult is it to console a child? Don't give me excuses!"

Suddenly, Birbal started crying and acting like a child. When Akbar tried to calm him down, Birbal demanded, "Father, I want a cow!"

Understanding Birbal's plan, Akbar ordered his men to bring a cow. However, Birbal started crying again and said, "Father, I want milk!"

Akbar ordered his men to milk the cow and give it to Birbal. Birbal had some of the milk and started crying again. Akbar was frustrated and asked, "What do you want now?"

Birbal replied, "Now please put the milk back into the cow."

Akbar laughed and said, "I give up, Birbal! You're right. It is tough to soothe a kid."

The Fastest Horse

Birbal once reached Akbar's court looking extremely tired. When Akbar asked him the reason, Birbal said, "My wife and children have gone to meet my in-laws. They took my chariot. So, I walked to the palace."

Akbar immediately ordered the manager of his stable to send the fastest horse in the stable to Birbal. The stable manager disliked Birbal, so he sent a weak and sick horse to Birbal's house. The horse was so ill that it died the same night. Birbal had to walk to reach the royal court again the next day.

Akbar asked him, "You are now in possession of the fastest horse we have, why are you late again then?"

Birbal replied, "Your Majesty, the horse was so fast that it reached heaven in just one night."

Akbar realised the mischief of the stable manager and punished him. He gifted Birbal a new and fast horse for travelling.

The Real Master

One day, two men came to Akbar's court arguing with each other. The first man said, "I am a merchant, and I had to travel to a different kingdom to expand my business. This man is my servant. I trusted him with my house in my absence. However, he stole my money and is now claiming that he is the real owner of my house."

The second man protested, "He's an imposter, *jahanpanah!* I am the real owner of the house, and he's trying to steal it from me."

Perplexed, Akbar asked Birbal to intervene. Birbal sternly said, "I can read minds and I know who is lying."

He then looked at the guard and thundered, "Execute the servant!"

The guard was confused, but he still took out his sword and moved forward. Fearing that he had been discovered, the second man fell upon Akbar's feet and started begging for mercy.

Akbar sent the servant to prison and praised Birbal's intelligence.

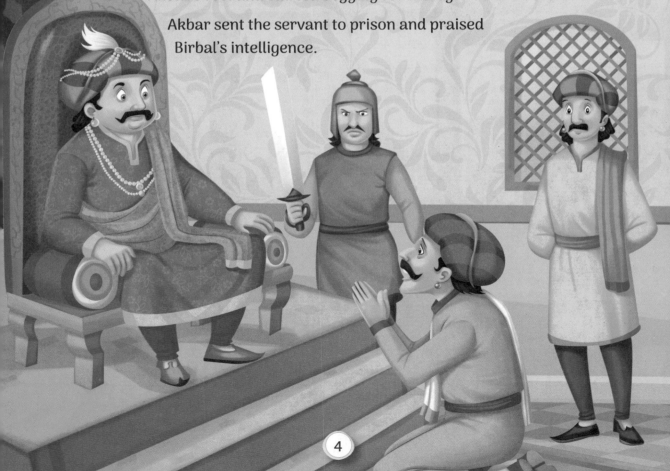

The Red Hot Test

One day, a man approached Emperor Akbar and said, "Your Majesty! This man, Hasan, has stolen my wife's necklace. Ask him to hold a hot iron rod in his hand. If he's honest, the deities won't let his hand burn."

Akbar agreed and ordered Hasan to take the test the next day. Worried, Hasan went to Birbal's house and asked for his help. Birbal came up with a plan. The next day, Hasan appeared in the court and said, "I insist that the rich man take the test first, since he is the one accusing me of this crime. If he isn't lying, the red hot iron rod won't hurt him either."

The rich man panicked and suggested that he might be mistaken. Akbar realised that the rich man was lying. As a punishment, he asked him to give the necklace to Hasan.

The Devotion of God

One day, Emperor Akbar asked Birbal, "Why does God always come to rescue his devotees himself? Why can't he send his servants?"

Birbal asked for some time to answer Akbar's question. In the meantime, he got a wax statue of Akbar's grandson created. He then asked the prince's caretaker to take it to the lake and wait for his signal. When Birbal and Akbar came to the lake, Birbal nodded to the caretaker. She dropped the statue into the lake.

Not knowing about Birbal's ploy, Akbar immediately jumped into the lake to save his grandson, but soon realised that it was a mere statue.

Birbal then asked Akbar, "*Huzoor*, you have many servants at your service. Why did you jump into the lake yourself?"

Akbar replied, "I love my grandson! I wanted to personally ensure his safety."

Birbal smiled and said, "God loves his devotees too, and hence He always comes to their rescue."

A List of Four Fools

Emperor Akbar once asked Birbal to make a list of four of the greatest fools in his kingdom. Birbal immediately left the court to fulfil his task. On his way, he saw a man who was riding a horse, while carrying wooden logs on his own head, as he didn't want to overload his horse. Next, he met a man who had raised his hands in the air to remember the correct dimensions of a vessel, rather than carrying the vessel to the market. He presented both the fools in the court.

But Akbar was not happy and complained, "Birbal, I asked you to find four of the greatest fools. However, you brought only two."

Birbal replied, "Your Majesty, The third fool is you, for assigning such a stupid task; and the fourth is me, for doing this task."

Akbar couldn't control his laughter upon hearing Birbal's witty response.

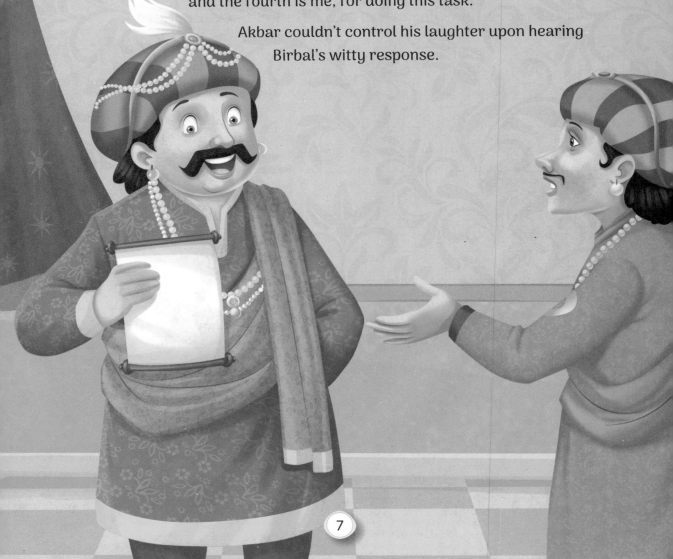

The Miraculous Saint

One day, Akbar was offended by a joke Birbal cracked. He roared, "Birbal! Get out of my court! I banish you from my city and kingdom. If I see you again, I shall have you executed."

Following Akbar's orders, Birbal immediately left the court. Several weeks went by, and Akbar started missing Birbal. He sent his spies in all directions but could not find him. Soon, a holy saint, along with his two disciples, arrived at Akbar's court. The disciples claimed that their teacher was a great scholar and could perform all sorts of miracles. Akbar was intrigued by this saint. He asked his courtiers to ask the saint the most challenging questions to check his brilliance. All of the Akbar's courtiers started asking difficult questions to the saint. To everybody's surprise, the saint answered each one of those accurately.

Akbar was impressed with the saint's replies, and finally, it was his turn to ask a question. He said, "Can you tell me who is the greatest enemy of an emperor?"

The saint replied, "It's his poor sense of humor."

Akbar asked several more questions, and the saint answered all of them to his satisfaction. Finally, Akbar said, "I hear you can also perform miracles. Can you present my ex-minister Birbal before me?"

The saint replied, "Of course, I can!"

Saying this, the saint started to remove his beard and the wig from his head. Within no time, the saint had transformed into Birbal. Akbar's eyes brightened to see his dear minister. Akbar immediately hugged Birbal and asked him to rejoin the royal court. Birbal thanked Akbar and resumed his duties as a minister.

The Elephant's Footprint

Emperor Akbar loved his queen dearly. When she asked him to make her brother the *diwan* of his kingdom, he couldn't refuse. Akbar asked Birbal to step down from the post and announced that his brother-in-law was the new *diwan*. One day, Akbar and his new *diwan* were travelling when Akbar noticed the footprints of his elephant and thought of a plan to test his brother-in-law's intelligence.

He said, "I want you to guard this footprint for three days."

The new *diwan* was surprised to receive such a request, but he agreed to follow Akbar's orders. He spent three days and nights around the footprint and informed Akbar of his success on the fourth day. Akbar was now sure that his brother-in-law wasn't suited for the job of the *diwan*. Akbar then called Birbal and assigned the same task to him. Birbal erected an iron poll near the footprint and tied a fifty-meter-long rope to the pole. He then announced, "By the emperor's orders, we need to

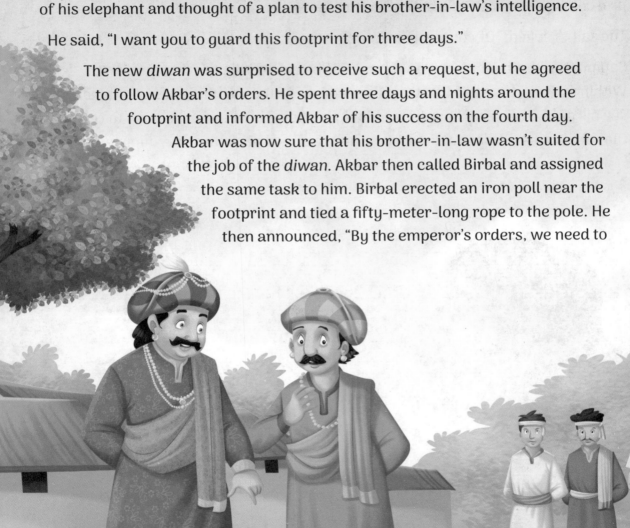

protect this footprint. Hence, we'll be demolishing all the houses that lie within a fifty-meter radius of this footprint."

The villagers panicked and offered to protect the footprint day and night. Birbal then said, "Alright! We will not destroy the houses, if you agree to protect this footprint."

The villagers agreed and erected a fence around the footprint. Birbal then said, "I shall be back after three days."

Birbal went back to the royal court and explained to Akbar how he had managed to ensure that the footprint would remain untouched. Akbar said to his brother-in-law, "Birbal has accomplished the task faster and more efficiently with his innovative approach. You are not fit for this job."

Akbar then re-appointed Birbal as his *diwan*.

Akbar and the Saint

Years of his reign had made Akbar a little arrogant as his courtiers always tried to flatter him and agreed with everything he said.

One day, Akbar was strolling in his royal garden when he bumped into a saint, who was lying on the ground. Akbar was furious and said, "How dare you enter my garden? Get up at once!"

The saint turned around and asked, "Oh! So, is this your garden?"

Akbar replied, "Of course, it is! This garden, its roses, their fragrance, the river, its water, this palace, this city, and even this kingdom belongs to me."

The saint questioned him again, "But I wonder, who was its owner before your birth?"

Akbar replied patiently, "Before me, all these things belonged to my father, and before him, they belonged to my grandfather."

The saint became excited and said, "I got it! It means, one day, all of this will belong to your child and then your grandchild."

Akbar was intrigued by the behaviour of the saint and replied, "Yes, indeed!"

The saint then asked, "So, basically, you are like a custodian, just like the innkeeper of an inn. Isn't this world like an inn, and people are mere travelers who stay in it? You come to this world and somethings belong to you, but when you leave, the same things belong to someone else. This means that nothing is ours. Everything remains here."

Akbar's replied, "I am impressed with your philosophy. Who are you?"

The saint removed his beard and wig. Akbar was surprised to see Birbal standing in front of him. He said with excitement, "I loved our discussion, Birbal. Let's go inside and discuss more philosophy."

The Bag of Gold

An old woman once decided to embark on a pilgrimage. She had a few gold coins as her savings. She kept the gold coins inside a small pouch and sewed the pouch. She then went to a respected judge and said, "Sir, I am going on a pilgrimage. Please take care of my bag. I shall collect the bag from you after I return."

The judge agreed to keep the bag safe until the old woman returned. A few months later, the woman returned, and the judge returned the pouch to her. The woman cut the stitches on the bag and looked inside. She was shocked to see a few pebbles inside the pouch. The woman accused the judge of stealing her money.

The judge harshly replied, "I did not open your bag. I am a wealthy man, and I don't need your money. Stop lying, or I will throw you inside a prison."

The woman was devastated after losing her entire savings. She went to the royal court and after narrating the entire incident, she pleaded to Akbar, "*Jahanpanah*, please give me justice. The judge should be punished for his actions."

The judge was an influential person, and Akbar did not want to punish him without any proof. He asked Birbal to investigate the matter further. Birbal examined the pouch and asked the woman, "Did you notice any tampering in the stitches on the bag when the judge gave it back to you?"

The woman replied, "No."

Birbal asked the lady to come back after two days. Later in the day, Birbal said to Akbar, "*Huzoor*, before going to sleep tonight, please cut your bedsheet into two."

Akbar was intrigued, but he agreed to Birbal's plan. He cut one of the sheets into two and went to sleep.

By noon next day, Akbar was surprised to see that the torn bedsheet had been sewn together so perfectly that he could not find any cut marks. Akbar told Birbal about the incident. Birbal summoned the servants and asked them about the person who had sewn the bedsheet.

The servants took Birbal to a tailor's shop. Birbal showed the old woman's bag to the tailor there and asked him, "Do you remember this bag?"

The tailor replied, "Yes. A few weeks ago, a judge from our town came to me. He asked me to remove the stitches on the bag. After removing gold coins from the bag, he placed pebbles inside and asked me to stitch it up again."

Birbal reported the matter to the king. Akbar summoned the judge and asked him to return the gold coins to the old woman. Later, the judge was removed from his post and thrown inside a prison.